Rur

written by Susan Hughes
illustrated by Pauline Whimp

1

"Why won't you leave me alone?" Greg shouted at the boys. He yanked the pillow from his bunk and grabbed his day pack. "Well, how about I leave you alone then? Goodbye and good riddance!"

Furious, Greg quickly stalked down the path that wound between the bunk rooms and the main school buildings and led to the lake. It was a glorious twilight, the sun setting in a brilliant blaze, the full moon just rising, but Greg was too bothered to notice.

He had put up with
being bullied by these
boys for two weeks, but
that was enough: he
would refuse to allow
it to continue for one
more minute. He would
simply run away...
Except, unfortunately,
this wilderness school
was on an island – the
whole point of him being
here, according to his
Dad. "You'll experience
living in, and with,
nature," he had said.
Well, Greg now knew
that he couldn't cope
with nature, and so,
once he found a boat,
he would leave this
place and head back
to the city.

4

The sail boats were no use to him. Unlike the other boys, who all seemed to be natural in the outdoors, Greg couldn't sail, or horseback ride, or light a fire, or put up a tent: all reasons why he didn't fit in here. "You'll learn to love it, son," his father had said. "Just give it a chance."

But although he excelled at the school work as usual, in the first week he'd been unable to light a campfire, and in the second week he had almost stepped on a snake and then got lost on a hike.

Hey! A motor boat!

Greg hurried through the dark to the boat, tied alongside the dock with a single line. He pulled one end close, glimpsing a lifejacket and a pile of something else – blankets maybe? – at the other end.

Greg threw in his pillow and backpack, untied the line, and climbed in. He eyed the outboard motor nervously. Although he'd seen other boys start it – boys younger than him – it was one of the many skills he'd never learned.

Grateful for the moonlight, he twisted the control on the steering arm to "START", gripped the handle of the starting cord in his other hand, and pulled back. Nothing.

Too weak, he decided.

Greg tried again, and again, and again, pulling successively harder, quicker, until finally, success! The motor fired. Greg turned and sat facing forward, grateful that the boat's bow was pointed toward the mainland. When he cautiously twisted the control on the steering arm to "FORWARD", the boat moved steadily through the calm water. Greg felt a surge of achievement. He was actually driving a motor boat – he wasn't completely hopeless after all! – and when he reached the mainland – well, he'd figure out the rest then.

"You woke me up. So, where are we going?" It was a male voice, and then, stretching his arms and yawning, the young man himself appeared from the pile of blankets in the boat. "A moonlight cruise?" he added, matter-of-factly.

Greg gasped, almost falling out of the boat if not for his grip on the control stubbornly refusing to let go. "I'm...we're going to the mainland," he stammered. "Who...who are you?"

"Josh. And you?"

Josh, the senior year troublemaker, who all the boys had heard about! Sent here as a boarder six years ago from a juvenile detention home, and now in his final year, apparently able to survive alone for weeks in the woods, and yet everyone still talked about him behind his back.

After being teased with slurs like "uncoordinated" and "newbie" himself, Greg knew how bad that could feel.

"I'm Greg," he replied.

"It's so beautiful out here, so calm, that I sometimes sleep here under the stars," Josh explained. Then he paused. "But, hey, I suspect the gas tank in this boat is low. Not sure how far..." The motor sputtered and failed.

Greg sighed, his chin falling to his chest. What a disaster! He couldn't even manage to run away from school properly.

"Hey, here's an idea," Josh said, encouragingly. "There are two paddles here. If we each take one, it'll be slow but steady, but we'll make some headway."

He was right, Greg found, as the boys began to paddle. They were moving again, slowly but steadily.

"So why are we going to the mainland?" Josh asked.

Greg hesitated, and then his story poured out: the taunting and teasing, hating the outdoors, being so pathetic at wilderness skills.

Josh made a sympathetic noise, and they just kept paddling. The boat moved slowly, but the pull of the paddle through the water felt good on Greg's arms and it felt surprisingly peaceful on the lake. An hour, maybe two, passed, and Greg had lost all sense of direction, but he didn't care. He liked it out here, on the water and under the night sky.

When Greg saw the mainland emerge from the darkness, he
was almost sorry. But then he dropped his paddle and cried out
accusingly, "We're back at the island! Back at boarding school!"
He glared at Josh. "I trusted you!"

"Exactly," agreed Josh, nodding. "That's why we're here. I
couldn't just let you head off to the city without giving this place
a fair chance."

"It'd be a shame if you left so soon, just when you're getting some sense of the place, getting the hang of driving a boat. With some boating lessons from me, you might become quite an expert," Josh added.

Despite his anger, Greg couldn't help feeling a glow of pride at the compliment.

"Also you might find you like the outdoors, the lake, the whole wilderness experience. I bet your room mates haven't reported you missing yet, which means that I, the rebel," Josh grinned, "could probably help you to sneak back in without getting into any trouble."

Greg considered briefly, then smiled. "Okay," he agreed, because, amazingly, it seemed that he did want to stay. His Dad and Josh might be right: maybe this wilderness boarding school could turn out alright, after all.

24